No Substitutions

Strange Matter™
titles in Large-Print Editions:

No Substitutions

Marty M. Engle

Gareth Stevens Publishing
MILWAUKEE

For a free color catalog describing Gareth Stevens' list of high-quality books and
multimedia programs, call 1-800-542-2595 (USA) or 1-800-461-9120 (Canada).
Gareth Stevens Publishing's Fax: (414) 225-0377.
See our catalog, too, on the World Wide Web: http://gsinc.com

Library of Congress Cataloging-in-Publication Data

Engle, Marty M.
    No substitutions / by Marty M. Engle.
        p. cm. -- (Strange matter)
    Summary: Curtis and Shelly find their lives in danger when they encounter
a sinister substitute teacher hiding a book about werewolves.
    ISBN 0-8368-1667-6 (lib bdg.)
    [1. Werewolves--Fiction. 2. Substitute teachers--Fiction. 3. Teachers--Fiction.
4. Schools--Fiction. 5. Horror stories.] I. Title. II. Series.
PZ7.E716No 1996
[Fic]--dc20   96-19602

This edition first published in 1996 by
Gareth Stevens Publishing
1555 North RiverCenter Drive, Suite 201
Milwaukee, Wisconsin 53212 USA

© 1995 by Front Line Art Publishing. Under license from Montage Publications,
a division of Front Line Art Publishing, San Diego, CA.

Printed in the United States of America

1 2 3 4 5 6 7 8 9 99 98 97 96

TO OUR FAMILIES
&
FRIENDS
(You know who you are)

With one springing leap the wolf overtook the wild rabbit. The wolf's speed amazed me. That rabbit never knew what hit it. Both animals flew amazingly fast across the field. The grass behind them blurred into a streak, then WHAM! In a flash of claws and bone-white teeth, the rabbit met his doom.

We couldn't see how much blood splattered the grisly scene because of the grass.

We could hear it though, wet sounds between the cracks and crunching. That's the way it always goes in those lame nature films. They never show the good stuff.

With a click, the lights flooded the biology class in room 112, Fairfield Junior High, eighth grade. My eyes stung and I stifled a yawn. The bell would ring any moment and Mr. Mayfield tried to remind us of our reading assignments before we stampeded to the door.

Above the noise, I could hear only the shuffle of papers, the scooting of chairs and my name being called in the distance.

"CURTIS! CURTIS CHATMAN!" the excited voice demanded.

The voice belonged to Shelly Miller, one of my best friends. She gets excited easily and plays with her ponytail when you talk to her. She can be pretty frustrating at times. She keeps up with me in almost everything and gets bored quick, like me.

"You'll never believe it, but guess what!" she blurted.

"What?" My eyes stayed half-closed as I tried to shake the groggy feeling from my head.

"Fine. You could at least pretend to be interested." She flipped her ponytail at me and spun as if she were going to leave. I knew she wouldn't. It twists her heart to know something I don't and not tell me.

I just had to wait.

"Okay. I'll tell you anyway." She turned back around, her eyes lit with excitement.

I shot up in my seat.

"Mr. Jackson isn't here today. We have a substitute," she whispered.

"YES!" I shouted. Best news I'd had all day. Mr. Jackson is the most boring teacher in the entire school. Shelly and I have him after lunch in the late afternoon. After lunch and late in the afternoon isn't the best time for history class.

Mr. Jackson keeps the windows closed so it stays warm and muggy in the room and, even then, wears a sweater.

His voice never varies and he never laughs. He slowly marches up and down the aisles to make sure we are paying attention. It is the hour where time stands painfully still.

For a moment I wondered about Mr. Jackson's absence, then I realized I didn't care. A more important question presented itself.

"Who's the substitute?"

With Mrs. Likens, we would spend the afternoon listening to pleas for silence and spreading disorder across the room.

With Coach Thomas, we would endure an afternoon of perfect posture and math puzzles.

Mrs. Fortune on the other hand . . .

"It's Mrs. Fortune!" Shelly exclaimed.

"EXCELLENT!" Mrs. Fortune would line us up and march us down to the library for the rest of the afternoon.

We could read any book we wanted as long as we read. No problem with Shelly and me. We would go straight to our favorite section, mysteries.

Shelly tugged me toward the door so fast I hardly had time to grab my notebook, my most prized possession. It contains all the artwork I have drawn since first grade, from cover to cover. Mostly monsters but other things, too. It even saved me from a fight once.

On that day, Kyle Banner decided he didn't like me and was going to show me how much after school. Fortunately, he saw the picture of a werewolf I drew on my notebook during Mr. Mayfield's boring afternoon film and he loved it.

He even asked me to draw one on his notebook. He watched in awe as I sketched and shaded and completed the monstrous master-piece before his very eyes. Since then he hasn't given me any trouble.

I kept my notebook from sliding as Shelly tugged me out the door and down the hall.

She can get really pushy sometimes. I like

that, though. If I can't think of anything to do, she can. When she's bored, I usually come up with something.

Shelly and I arrived last at Mr. Jackson's door. A flood of kids washed into the room as the bell sounded. No problem. Mrs. Fortune didn't care if we weren't in our seats when the bell rang.

The bell stopped.

We walked to the rear of the line and waited our turn. No big deal.

Shelly tossed her ponytail back. "What a great way to end the day."

Wrong.

I saw him first.

We both swallowed hard.

It wasn't Mrs. Fortune.

Sitting in Mr. Jackson's seat, where Mrs. Fortune should have been, sat a man I had never seen before.

He had white-blond hair in a bowl shape and piercing blue eyes. His eyebrows grew together over his nose. His smile seemed fake. His eyes stared fiercely at each student filing into the class.

"Who's that?" Shelly whispered.

"I have no idea." I hurried past her with a new urgency to get to my seat.

We all sat impatiently, trying to get a fix on this new person at the head of the class.

He sat and smiled at us. At first we gave forced smiles back, with a half-hearted grin here, a lop-sided smirk there. Kelly Dunway was trying way too hard to smile, showing all her teeth like she was in pain.

The silence loomed. Who would crack first? Who held the power in the room? The tension mounted. These first crucial moments always told the tale.

We looked around at each other. No one said anything. The usual Substitute Teacher Terrorizers sat looking as puzzled as the rest of us. No one dared move or even breathe.

The substitute seemed to sense when we reached the breaking point.

He slapped the desk and shot to his feet. He chuckled and mumbled to himself. Friend or enemy, we couldn't yet tell.

"Good afternoon, class. My name is Stacy Calhoun."

He said his name like he was a star or something. Like we should know him from television.

"Stacy Calhoun." He rocked on his toes as he said his name again and stared at the ceiling, as if hearing silent cheering and applause.

We nodded in approval of his name.

That's the only thing we could figure he wanted.

"Have you kids ever heard of me?" He

peered at us, waiting for an answer.

We looked at each other and then to the floor. This guy was creepy. He must have actually thought we had heard his name before. Probably he was some famous prison warden or army captain.

I felt a quick poke to my shoulder. I turned slightly to see Shelly tapping me with a folded piece of notebook paper.

I reached carefully over my shoulder, never taking my eyes off the warden, and grabbed the note. I had it in my lap in less than half a second.

Too slow.

In three giant steps, he hovered over me, his eyes huge and staring.

I stifled a yelp as his huge hand plucked the note from my lap.

I stared up at his face and noticed a very fine layer of blond hair, on his nose, on his forehead, everywhere! Even on his eyelids. Weird, to say the least.

"I held the proud title of star quarterback for Fairfield High, three years running, back in the early 1970's. I substitute teach now."

Oh, no. And I bet that thought echoed in

every single kid in class.

"You no doubt believe that my reflexes have slackened with age. Enough to give you leeway for note-passing, airplane sailing, rubberband flipping, gum chewing or name calling. Unfortunately, you will be surprised by my keen eyesight and my acute hearing."

He moved away from my desk toward the back of the class. I didn't like him behind me even more than I didn't like him in front of me. I really didn't like his King of the Universe tone of voice, either.

"Your scheduled substitute teacher, Mrs. Fortune, couldn't make it today so I am filling in. I had a lesson plan but I've decided not to use it." He said it as if he had done us a huge favor, which he probably had.

He walked down the center aisle like a king. No one said a word. No one whispered. I'm not sure if anyone breathed. He walked up to Mr. Jackson's desk and stood with his back to us for a moment. He had everyone's attention and he knew it.

"What would Mrs. Fortune have done with you for the rest of the day?"

Shelly's hand shot up. She had a look on

her face I had seen before. The same look she gave Kyle Banner before she punched him out.

Stacy Calhoun's ears perked back and his head raised slightly and cocked, like an animal that heard something behind it.

"You, the little note-passer?" he called.

He didn't turn around. How did he know Shelly raised her hand? How did he see her?

"We would have gone to the library for the rest of the day," Shelly said. It sounded more like a demand than a statement.

He turned around slowly with the same smile as before.

"Well then! Let's go the library! Single file. Now."

A huge clamor erupted as chairs slid and kids lined up at the door.

Shelly and I stood last in line. We took our time. The library wouldn't be nearly as much fun as we had planned. Not with Mr. Stacy Calhoun in charge.

"I want you all to march straight to the library. No talking. Anyone who steps out of line will be very sorry. Move out."

The stunned students started forward in silence and in perfect line.

Stacy Calhoun did it. He achieved total control in a record amount of time. Our class, with the reputation for being uncontrollable, particularly with substitute teachers, became as docile as pet dogs.

We almost made it out the door when we felt his huge hands on our shoulders.

"Could I speak to you two for a moment?" he said.

"What are your names?" he asked.

I struggled to reply but Shelly beat me to the punch, as usual.

"Shelly Miller," she announced, staring straight at him. I could never look at adults when I spoke to them. Sometimes I hated even talking to older people.

"And yours?" he said. His gaze darted to me. His eyes had a strange look about them now. A striking blue before, but now they appeared silvery.

I looked down quickly. "Curtis Chatman," I said staring at the floor tile. I don't think they ever mopped the floor at this school.

"I wonder if I could get you two to help me carry some things down to the library." He smiled and turned to the desk.

We didn't move. Shelly nudged me and tried to mouth out something. I couldn't understand her. I felt like a prisoner awaiting sentencing.

He turned, holding two large cardboard boxes and held them out, one in each huge hand.

Our arms nearly broke when we took the incredibly heavy boxes. How could he hold them in his hands like that? We could barely lift them. We set them on the floor with a loud thump.

He looked down at us with a forced smile. A punishment for passing notes. That's what his fake smile told us.

"Can you manage them?" he asked. No mere question, but a challenge.

Shelly looked mad and grabbed her box, tugging it up to her knee where she slid her hands beneath it. She would manage them all right. She'd pull her arms out of their sockets before she would admit defeat.

"No problem," I muttered.

I lifted my box and shuffled for the door as best I could, Shelly right behind me.

"Take them down to the library and sit quietly with the rest of the class. I'll be there momentarily."

He stopped us with a snap and a command.

"Everyone will be quiet and seated or they will be very sorry."

I felt his stare on the back of my head as Shelly and I pushed through the doors and staggered down the hall toward the library.

We paused at the top of the stairs. We looked at each other and at the heavy boxes we carried, each box taped shut.

"Why did he make us do this? He knew these were too heavy for us!" Shelly growled.

"Punishment for passing notes," I said. "He gets an A for originality. He *asked* us to carry these stupid things. He didn't order us. We could have said no, you know."

"Why didn't you?"

"I don't know! Why didn't you?"

My arms were killing me already. I knew Shelly's must really be sore. She has a lot of energy but she's really not that strong.

"Why didn't he just send us to the principal or something? This isn't fair at all."

"By the way, what did your note say? I never had a chance to read it."

Shelly stopped and smiled.

"I was going to ask you what you thought were in these boxes."

We looked at each other and laughed, then set the boxes down on the top of the stairs with a thump.

I suppose I should have carried my box down the stairs as Stacy Calhoun had asked.

I didn't.

I kicked my box down to the first step and then the next. It would take awhile, but I wouldn't break my back.

"Not what he intended," Shelly giggled.

A few minutes later, a final kick placed our boxes on the last step. The hallway stood empty, no teachers to help us and no students to laugh.

"Great. You think we can kick them on down to the library?" Shelly grumbled.

"Nah. We better carry them. My box is about to cave in." Cardboard boxes get pretty ragged after a hundred kicks and about fifty stairsteps.

I kicked the box again. That's what Stacy Calhoun got for his stupid punishment. A beat-up box, courtesy of Curtis Chatman.

With a groan, we bent to pick the boxes up. I could feel my arms stretch about a foot as I lifted.

Shelly got a horrified look on her face. She gasped.

"Oh no, Curt! You forgot your notebook! It's back in class!"

I couldn't believe it. I'd left it behind when I picked up this stupid box.

"Wait here! I'll be back in a second!" I shouted.

I shot up the stairs, skipping steps as I went. I left the stupid box with Shelly.

I started around the upstairs corner, and jogged all the way up to Mr. Mayfield's biology class, heading toward Mr. Jackson's history.

I couldn't let Mr. Mayfield see me. He hated tardiness and people without hall passes. He wouldn't care if I left my *head* in my last class. I was supposed to be in my *next* class.

As luck would have it, Mr. Mayfield had a free period. He would either be eating his regular tunafish salad sandwich and coming up with his lesson plan for tomorrow or he would still be rewinding the film from his last class. He had problems with that sometimes.

As I sneaked past his door, I heard something that made my blood run cold.

"I told you NO! How many times do I have to tell you!" Mr. Mayfield cried out.

That's all I heard before another voice hushed him. I hugged the wall next to Mr. Mayfield's door. I had to sneak on past but my curiosity had peaked.

Mr. Mayfield had never even raised his voice before as far as I knew. Now he yelled and screamed at somebody in his class! It must have been a bad situation for him to get so upset.

I took a big gulp of air, held it and peeked through the tiny glass window of the closed door.

The fluorescent lights in the room flickered on and off, threatening to go out. The projector still whirred. The film left in the reel clicked over on itself, over and over.

I saw them.

A large hand held Mr. Mayfield in his chair. The hand belonged to Stacy Calhoun.

His other hand curled up behind him in a large fist.

It pulled back to punch Mr. Mayfield! I

couldn't believe it!

I found my mouth opening before I could stop it. Paralyzed with shock, I couldn't force a sound out, not even a squeak.

Mr. Calhoun's fist came sailing around his giant body and slammed into the chair beside Mr. Mayfield's head.

Mr. Mayfield leaped to his feet and backed toward the projector. His legs looked like they would buckle beneath him at any moment.

"There is no way I am going to join you! You can do whatever you want, say whatever you want to say, but I won't!" Mr. Mayfield yelled.

Mr. Calhoun turned and I got a good look at his face, all twisted and a deep shade of red. I don't think I had ever seen anyone that furious.

He started toward Mr. Mayfield who was stepping behind a large dissection table. The table was covered in bottles, beakers, live frogs croaking loudly inside their jars and...

dissection knives.

My heart jumped to my throat.

Mr. Mayfield and Mr. Calhoun circled the table, never taking their eyes off of each other.

"Come now, Mr. Mayfield. Won't you

reconsider?" Mr. Calhoun placed his hands carefully on the table. The frogs croaked loudly and jumped frantically in their jars.

Mr. Mayfield sweated nervously. He shook. A look of determination pinched his reddened face.

"I said no and I mean no!" he finally cried.

Stacy stared at Mr. Mayfield for a moment, then picked up a dissection knife.

The frogs went crazy.

I wanted to scream. I felt my heart pound and my legs grow weak.

Mr. Calhoun held the knife.

My face was fully in that little window now. From inside, it must have looked like my head sat on a shelf, staring in.

Mr. Calhoun looked from the gleaming knife to Mr. Mayfield and then to...

me.

A jolt of terror surged through my body and I froze.

He looked straight at the little window in the door and saw me. His eyes glinted and locked me in place.

I stared back, terrified.

His gaze turned to Mr. Mayfield.

He quickly capped the knife with a small plastic cover and shoved it in his pocket.

"You had your chance. Now it's too late. You should have joined me. You should have come with me. It could have been just like the old days."

Mr. Mayfield seemed as terrified as I was.

"Go on. Check your hand." Stacy said coolly.

Mr. Mayfield slowly brought his fist in front of his face. He pressed his fist hard against his forehead and started to open it.

Stacy smiled as Mr. Mayfield's face flooded with terror. Mr. Mayfield's fingers unfurled and his opened hand shook.

The frogs went wild in their jars.

I could see that something marked Mr. Mayfield's outstretched palm!

Something terrible.

I ducked behind the corner at the top of the stairs. I heard the door to the biology class slam into the wall. My heart nearly jumped from my chest.

Mr. Mayfield didn't see me as he ran past, holding his palm to his chest as if it were cut.

My head ached and I broke a cold sweat as the realization hit me. I had never seen two teachers fight before. What should I do? Who should I tell?

I didn't have time to think about it. I heard a second set of footsteps heading toward me down the hall.

It had to be Mr. Calhoun.

I couldn't let him find me because I had no idea what he would do. The footsteps came closer.

I flew down the stairs. My heart pounded. I knew he followed close behind.

I saw Shelly standing at the bottom of the stairs with her arms crossed, next to the two heavy boxes.

Someone stood next to her!

Coach Dawson! All right! My tennis instructor! Mom had signed me up for lessons with Coach Dawson over the summer. I really liked him. Tough but not too tough. He saw me coming down the stairs and waved. A feeling of relief washed through me. My life had been narrowly spared at the last moment.

I waved back at my rescuer and bounced down the last three steps confident that Mr. Calhoun wouldn't dare touch me with another teacher around.

"Hey, coach!" I called cheerfully. Then it occurred to me. Mr. Calhoun took care of Mr. Mayfield very easily.

A gnawing dread started to chew my stomach. My brief sense of security vanished as quickly as it had come.

"It's about time! Did you get lost or what?" Shelly said.

"Hey, Curtis, these are pretty heavy boxes

for you guys to be carrying around. Whose are they?" Coach Dawson scratched his orange mop of hair under his bright red cap.

"They belong to the new substitute," I said, trying to disguise the quake in my voice.

"He's a real jerk, Coach Dawson. He knew we couldn't carry these heavy things all the way to the library." Shelly's nose wrinkled in a sign of true disdain.

"Who?" Coach Dawson asked.

An ominous shadow loomed over us. It blocked out all the light coming from the stair-case window. I didn't have to look.

I knew who it was.

"Why, Mr. Mayfield! Is something wrong?" Coach Dawson sounded surprised.

I turned to look. Mr. Mayfield hurried down the stairs toward us, his hands in his pockets and a worried expression on his pale, round face.

"Oh hi, Coach Dawson. I'm just a little under the weather today, that's all. Hello Shelly...Curtis."

Mr. Mayfield stared at me with a strange urgency. I could see he wanted to tell me something about what happened between him and

Stacy Calhoun. He knew I'd seen them. He seemed shaken, almost terrified.

"Sorry you feel bad, Doug. You heading out?" Coach Dawson offered his hand. Mr. Mayfield only looked at him and kept his hands in his pockets.

"Yes. I have a few errands to run. Then I'm going home for the rest of the day." Mr. Mayfield hurried past us.

"Not much of the day left," Coach Dawson replied.

Mr. Mayfield didn't look back.

"Hope you feel better soon, Doug!" Coach Dawson called after him.

Mr. Mayfield disappeared through the door to the teacher's lounge.

"That's odd. Well, I guess I'll help you two Samsons with these crates."

"Thanks, Coach Dawson, but I think I can manage mine all by myself." Shelly proudly lifted her box with a huff. It almost slipped but Coach Dawson straightened it for her.

She swaggered on down the hallway, her ponytail flipping from side to side.

Coach Dawson looked down at me.

"How 'bout you Curt? Need some help?"

I watched as Shelly turned to glare at me. If I accepted Coach Dawson's help, I'd never hear the end of it. Never.

"Sure. That thing's too heavy for me. I admit it," I said with a grin.

Coach Dawson got a big laugh out of that. He grabbed the box with one hand and then, clearly surprised by the weight, used two.

"This thing's heavier than it looks." As he started down the hall, I saw our school mascot on the back of his bright yellow jacket, the grey timber wolf.

Suddenly I heard Mr. Calhoun's voice behind me.

"A little late getting to the library, Curtis?" The voice curled around me like a snake. A cold shiver traveled through me.

I didn't turn around. Cold fear pushed me forward, but I half expected a hand on my shoulder to stop me or something.

Nothing. He didn't do anything, say anything. No sound. A chill wind whipped down the empty hall.

I took another step and felt hot breath on my neck.

Okay, I forced myself to turn and look.

I knew it. Nothing there. He had vanished, but how? Nothing down that hall but a scuffed up floor and hundred year old wads of gum. No doors had slammed and I'd heard no footsteps.

A blinding dread and a flash of fright sent me hurtling down the hall to catch up to Coach Dawson.

We entered the library together.

All the kids from my class ran amok
through the library. I couldn't believe the commotion!

Stuff flew everywhere! Mr. Dawson looked
around in disbelief. He turned his head in time
to catch a paper plane in the eye. Ouch. My class
hadn't earned their reputation for substitute-
busting for no reason. Any other time, and I
would have beamed with pride.

Not this time.

To my horror, I saw the box drop from
Coach Dawson's hands.

It seemed to fall in slow motion.

I watched as it tumbled. He frantically
grabbed at it, bumping it and twisting it in the
air. His desperate attempts only seemed to make
the box more determined to hit the ground. Boy,

did it hit the floor. It hit so hard it broke open. That's when the bugs poured out!

HUNDREDS of roaches and spiders streamed from the overturned box and scrambled across the floor!

My stomach lurched and heaved as the carpet of bugs rose ankle deep!

Everyone froze as the insects scurried over their shoes, and up their socks. The girls and boys screamed as they felt hairy little legs crawl up their shirts and into their hair. Poor Piggy Steiner had been crawling under the library tables pinching girls when a wave of bugs flooded over him.

He screamed for a full two minutes before Coach Dawson pulled him up. The coach brushed him off as best he could and yelled for silence.

No good. Shrieks and cries filled the library as the kids scrambled over each other for the door. Beneath their feet, the bugs popped, snapped and opened like peanut shells.

I saw Shelly laughing hysterically, perched on top of the card catalog. Shelly actually liked bugs, unlike most girls I know. She liked them enough to own a pet spider, an ant farm and two centipedes named "Flash" and "Speedy."

Coach Dawson started after the panicking crowd outside. He slammed through the door, barking at the kids to settle down.

The bugs disappeared almost as soon as they hit the floor. I saw the last few stragglers slide under some bookcase. Then they too vanished.

I jumped down and so did Shelly. We didn't care about the chaos outside the door or the dozens of smeared and splattered black spots on the floor.

We had to see the package that had burst open when it hit the floor. At least we would see what secrets one of the boxes held.

We drew closer, neither of us saying a word. Neither of us dared.

Shelly and I looked at each other, too nervous to say anything.

I reached for the crumpled cardboard flaps of the overturned box.

Shelly beat me to it!

Her hand grabbed the cardboard flap and flipped it up.

We both jumped back expecting more bugs or something even worse, but nothing sprang out. So far so good.

We peered inside. It looked as if it hadn't seen the light of day in a hundred years! Shelly carefully reached in though the cobwebs, her hand buried in the box.

"I can't believe you carried that thing! Just imagine...those bugs waited in there while you were carrying it. It's a good thing..."

"SHUT UP, CURTIS!" she snapped.

She pulled something out. A book, covered in dust.

I grabbed the book away from her.

"HEY! I got it out, chicken. I get to look at it first." She grabbed it back with a sharp tug and scowled at me.

She blew the dust off and revealed the cover. I couldn't believe it.

Very cool.

I had read books like it before but this one was different altogether, I could tell.

Werewolves.
The Loup Garou and others.

I felt a strange tingle and a rush of excitement. It was solid leather and heavy.

On the cover, etched in silver, was a face split exactly in the middle, one side a man, the other a snarling wolf.

Usually I think that books on werewolves and monsters are cool, but not this time. The book radiated a weird energy. I could feel it as I stared.

I think Shelly had the same feeling because she started breathing heavily when she opened the first page.

We both knew that werewolves and vampires and all that stuff are make-believe. Junk you see in the movies or on TV that isn't real. We even knew how most of the effects for those shows were done. I had models and masks and so did Shelly.

I could recite the lines from "The Wolfman" by heart, the old black and white movie with Lon Chaney, Jr.

This was different, entirely.

We had a book on the real thing.
Deep down, I knew it.

Shelly slammed it shut, her eyes wide and scared.

"We have to get out of here. This thing is real," she said.

"What?" I still couldn't believe it. I had to play it cool no matter what my brain told me. "Give me a break! That stuff isn't real. It's a phony."

Shelly only looked at me.

"Okay. It's real. Let's get out of here." I had to admit I felt a growing panic, myself.

"What about the other box?" she asked quietly.

"Where did you put it?"

"It's over there...AIIIIIIII!" Shelly screamed, grabbing her mouth.

Sitting on the librarian's desk was the box and right behind it sat Mr. Calhoun, a smile on his face as he leaned forward slowly.

"A little light reading?" he asked, his teeth bared to the gums. "Bring that over here, if you please, and be quick about it!"

At that moment, Coach Dawson bolted into the room, his finger of guilt extended and eager to point at someone.

"All right, now what the...?" he didn't have time to finish, and we didn't have time to reply.

A blur of movement and a gust of air, and Mr. Calhoun held us up by the backs of our shirts.

"It seems, Mr. Dawson, that we have a couple of insect collecting pranksters. Obviously I should have brought down my packages myself and chosen another penalty for my two little note-passers." The words flowed like silver off

Mr. Calhoun's tongue. I could see Mr. Dawson buying it completely.

I had to try to explain.

"But we..." I sputtered while I dangled from Mr. Calhoun's huge hand.

"Curtis, you neglected to tell me that you were being punished," Mr. Dawson said sternly.

"NO WAY!" Shelly yelled.

Coach Dawson sighed in disappointment.

"You know how I hate it when you guys don't pay attention in class," he concluded.

Game over. To Mr. Dawson, we'd committed the ultimate crime. Not paying attention in class ranked with armed bank robbery.

How were we going to get out of this?

We didn't get out of it.

Kenny Hedricks had over twenty spider bites on his scalp. Patty Carmike, allergic to ant bites, could plan on a week at the hospital.

In all, over thirty people suffered trauma from the insect incident and we bore the blame.

No trial. No hearing. No excuses. We stewed in solitary confinement with Mr. Dawson. A day's suspension seemed the least of our worries as the principal called our parents at work to come retrieve their delinquent children.

I had always thought the school system reserved suspension for future bank robbers, car thieves and 7-11 hold-up creeps who skulked around the back of social studies class.

I had no idea suspension waited for Shelly and me. A big, fat blemish on our permanent records. It would follow me the rest of my life. It would prevent me from getting into the college of my choice and probably be responsible for my career in can collecting and talking to statues in the park.

I had never been in trouble of this magnitude in my life! Now I could thank Stacy Calhoun...

the substitute.

SMACK! I punched my catcher's mitt again as I paced back and forth beneath the models of the B-2 bomber and Rodan that hung swaying from my ceiling.

I had cleaned my room, leaving nothing on the floor anywhere! I made sure everything found its place. It's something I do when I have to think. I guess by getting the clutter out of sight, I get the clutter out of my brain, too.

I kept seeing Stacy Calhoun's ugly, hairy face and those weird silvery eyes in my mind. I couldn't force the image out.

I paced to the window and stared down my street. The sky glowed with a purplish haze as twilight approached. I kept wishing that Shelly would call. She had a way of clearing up my head.

The phone rang loudly. It had to be Shelly. I grabbed it before Mom could.

"Hello?"

"Can you believe what is happening to us? Can you believe this!" Shelly huffed. I had a lot to tell Shelly about what I had seen, but I didn't want Mom to find out. I played it cool. I guessed I had about thirty seconds, so I started my act.

"This is so stupid. How? How did this happen to us? Why is that creep of a substitute out to get us?"

Mom picked up the phone and interrupted. I knew she would.

"Curtis, you have exactly two minutes. You are being punished, young man, so I want you off that phone and back on that essay just in case they decide to LET you back in school."

Ouch. That hurt. You see, Shelly and I had to write essays on the evil of our actions and how much shame we felt for it.

"You too, Shelly. I'll bet your mother doesn't know you're on the phone. I mean it, Curt. Two minutes," mother snapped.

Shelly didn't say anything.

Mom hung up the phone.

We could talk freely now.

39

"Curtis, how did he get to us so fast? I didn't even see him move! Why did he have all those bugs in his stupid box? Why did he have that book?" Shelly's mind raced faster than her mouth. I knew how she felt.

"I don't know, but I saw Mr. Mayfield and him in a fight. He almost punched Mayfield right in the face. Something about joining him like in the good old days, whatever that means. Anyway, Mayfield grabbed his hand and ran out. Something was burned into his palm."

"So that's why Mr. Mayfield looked so nervous and ran past us so fast. What could have been on his hand?"

"I didn't see, so I have no idea. Mr. Calhoun put it there, I'm sure of it. But he didn't touch him. He did it with his mind."

Silence on Shelly's end of the phone. Did she believe me? I'm not sure if I would have believed me.

"Oh come on. You don't think he has some kind of secret power or something do you?"

"I don't know, but you were the one who got so scared when you saw that book, remember?" I watched the sun go down through my thin, white curtains.

No reply.

"Shelly?"

"What do we do now? We're suspended for a day. That's serious. I've never been in trouble before in my life. It's all his fault. He's out to get us. I can't just do nothing."

Once, she got a "C" on a book report she did for Mrs. Dobson. She cornered the poor teacher on her way out of a faculty meeting. In front of the principal and the entire English department, she argued her way into a "B+". She took her school record very, very seriously.

I did too. I couldn't take this lying down either. We had to decide what to do next. My mind snapped to a plan of action.

"Let's find out what he said to Mr. Mayfield and what exactly was on Mr. Mayfield's palm," I said.

"If I get caught sneaking out, I'll never see daylight again."

I waited. She wouldn't be able to stand not going.

"All right. I'll meet you on the corner of Willow and Elm in one hour. Oh, hey. Curt?"

"Yeah?"

"Look at the mess we're in, because of one

stupid box."

"Yeah...your point is?" I knew what she would say and it made me sick to my stomach."

"What do you think is in the other box?"

10

It didn't take much to sneak out of the house. I slipped out my window, down onto the garage roof, down that steep angle to the drain, down the drain to the driveway, and from there to the tree lined street of Sycamore Way. It took me exactly twelve minutes to jog to the corner of Elm and Willow.

Shelly waited there. I could see her breath in the brisk air.

"Right on time," she said.

"Of course. You ready?"

"Let's go." She started up the street toward the freeway.

We talked excitedly. The words bounced out between quick steps and icy gulps of air.

"I don't get it. He moves too fast. Way too fast. He talks and you can't see him. He keeps massive insect zoos in cardboard boxes and reads a lot about things that howl in the night." I watched my feet hit every single crack in the sidewalk.

"He used to play football. I asked my Dad about him in between the yelling and cries of disbelief over his daughter's criminal behavior. Dad said Calhoun used to be the best. No one could stop him. He moved so fast you couldn't see him, and if you tried to tackle him, he'd jump over you like an animal. If he had the ball it was a guaranteed touchdown. People called him the "Beast of Fairfield High."

"Oh yeah?"

"He had a huge head." Shelly carefully avoided each crack in the sidewalk.

"I gathered that." The guy had two zip-codes for his ego alone.

"Apparently his whole family was jock. Everyone called his Dad 'The Beast', as well as his older brothers. There are pictures and trophies all over the high school. Dad seemed surprised to hear he actually came back to town after what happened in 1974."

I bit. "What happened?"

"Dad said they made him quit."

"Why?" We stopped at a red light. The crosswalk signal pressed with a click under my finger, the metal unusually cold.

"He crippled some guy for life. Broke his neck on the five yard line. "

I stopped abruptly and looked at Shelly as she slowly spun around the metal pole.

"Dad told me that Calhoun's speed amazed him. He said the poor guy never knew what hit him. They both ran so fast across the field that the grass under them blurred into a streak, then WHAM! A sickening crack and it was all over."

Like a rabbit, I thought. My heart sank as I recalled Mr. Mayfield's science film in gruesome detail.

"Dad said that Calhoun smiled and waved as the poor guy's stretcher slid into the ambulance. The crowd didn't make a sound but Calhoun's Dad and his brothers cheered and *howled* over the victory."

Calhoun bowed in my head, receiving imaginary cheers. The dissection knife gleamed in his hand. He stared at me with shimmering silver eyes.

"I guess they'll let anybody substitute

teach, these days," Shelly said.

We waited for the traffic signal to change. It had just turned yellow. Wait a minute. Yellow? It should have gone straight from red to green. Something must have been wrong with the light. No cars around, but I'd been in enough trouble that day. I'd wait for a walking signal.

"What a creep," I said, my hands in my pockets.

"He left town with his family a week later after some kind of trouble with his Dad. He's still a legend of sorts and an underground football hero. Dad said a lot of his friends *still* think of Calhoun as the greatest quarterback Fairfield ever saw. Now he's back."

"Your Dad *told* you all this?"

"Well, no...not exactly. I overheard him and Mom talking about it while I was stewing in my room. After they found out who got me in trouble, they almost believed my story."

"I wish I could say the same. I'm in the doghouse for good," I moped.

"Good choice of words," she joked.

"What do you mean by that?"

She just laughed.

"What happened to Calhoun's Dad?" I

asked staring at the light. An awfully long time to wait for a light to change. Very weird.

"He died last year. Dad thinks that's why Calhoun came back to Fairfield. To get away from his family."

Shelly also stared up at the light. It glowed a dingy yellow. The crossing signal remained a cold, dead black.

"What did his Dad do?" I asked, my attention more focused on the light than the question.

"He was the dog catcher."

The light refused to change.

11

The traffic light cast its sickly yellow glow on the cool night mist that drifted around it. We kept staring at it, willing it to change.

It didn't.

"What's up with that dumb light?" Shelly quaked. I could tell the light gave her the creeps, though she'd never admit it.

The light stayed yellow! The only light shining on the empty streets. No lights on in the houses and no car lights heading down the streets.

"Man, this is ridiculous! What's going on?" I felt a trickle of fear run down my neck.

The light remained yellow.

We looked around nervously.

A small breeze stirred the dead air but the light refused to sway. It didn't move a bit.

It shone through the mist with its dull, yellow glow.

Then I became aware of the parked cars.

Cars sat like abandoned shells everywhere. They lined the streets like tombstones, all silent and dark.

My pulse quickened as the feeling of being watched crept over me.

I heard something behind us. Not on the sidewalk but under a large moving van parked on the corner, right behind us.

"Did you hear that?" I whispered.

"Hear what?" Shelly whispered back.

Something crawled across the concrete under the van. I frantically looked behind me.

'THAT! Did you hear it?" My eyes locked onto the dark hulk of the moving van.

The whole van creaked and swayed as if something slid under it.

Shelly saw it too and without a word bolted across the street, light or no light!

"SHELLY!" I yelled and ran after her into the middle of the street.

Instantly two headlights sprang to life on a car on the opposite side of the street.

The car screeched forward, but its wheels

didn't turn! Smoke curled from the rubber as it screamed against the pavement!

Something howled, propelling the car toward us with its emergency brakes on!

Shelly screamed as the car lunged at her. I lunged too and knocked us both to the sidewalk.

The car stopped behind us in the middle of the crosswalk.

Shelly closed her eyes and screamed.

I turned and saw it.

A huge skulking figure with pointed dog-like ears removed its claws from the back of the car with a metallic groan. It turned to come after us, only a few steps away!

I couldn't see it well in the dark but I knew it would be on us in moments. I pulled Shelly to her feet and we ran.

The sound of my heartbeat echoed in my head in time to the rapid smack of my sneakers against the pavement.

I wouldn't look back no matter what. I couldn't be sure if Shelly had kept up with me. I lost track of her in the dark.

I felt sick to my stomach and guilty for not thinking more about Shelly's safety but in my mind I saw those claws pulling out of that car's bumper and that horrible, hairy figure outlined in the pale yellow of the traffic light. I couldn't stop for anything.

Shelly screamed.

I stopped at the overpass bridge so fast my legs gave out. I tumbled to the sidewalk and scraped my arm.

"CURTIS! PLEASE! I CAN'T KEEP UP!" Shelly screamed hysterically.

She fell beside me on the pavement, gasping for air.

"Curtis! What was that thing?" She was breathing so hard I could hardly understand her. I looked behind her and saw nothing following us. Whatever it was, we'd lost it.

"I don't know, but I could make a pretty good guess." I squinted, peering down the street. Nothing there. My arm started bleeding and stinging badly.

"That car almost killed me! He tried to push it into me!" She started crying.

"Hey, you're okay. Let's get out here. We better go on to Mr. Mayfield's."

Shelly started crying louder and shaking her head, "No way. I want to go home."

"We can't go back that way and Mr. Mayfield's house is closer. Come on, we haven't got much of a choice."

I pulled her from the street to a grassy area beside the road.

"Look, that could have been anything or anyone back there. After the day we've had, we probably just imagined that it looked like a...well, what we thought it was."

"Bull! It's Stacy Calhoun! He's trying to kill us!" Shelly argued, more angry than scared.

"Come on now. It's dark. That could have been some guy trying to push start his car or something. He left his emergency brakes on, and it got away from him in the dark, that's all."

Shelly fixed me with an icy stare. "He sure had terrific timing."

I couldn't argue with that, but I couldn't believe what had happened either. Could it have been a crazy substitute teacher trying to kill us or only a stupid guy with car trouble? I couldn't think straight. My legs trembled.

"Look, let's just go on to Mr. Mayfield's house and get our heads together. I need to wash my arm before it gets infected." I stuck it out for her approval. It dripped blood.

"Oh, gross. What did you do?" Shelly reached out to dab my arm with her finger.

"OW! That hurts!"

"You sure got it good. Okay. Let's get moving. Promise we'll go home right after, okay...and we'll go back a different way." She struggled to her feet.

I joined her. "It's a deal. We've probably only got an hour or so left before our parents check on us."

"Let's go," she said and stepped onto the bridge. The lights of the cars on the freeway below reflected on her pale pink jacket.

Mr. Mayfield's house, and hopefully the answers to our questions, waited across the freeway overpass and two more streets over.

If I had known then what the answers would be, I would have gone straight home.

Werewolf or no werewolf.

13

We stood nervously on the doorstep of a small, grey two-story house on Dogwood Avenue. Swallowing hard, I pressed the doorbell. I held my breath. No immediate response.

I breathed out and turned to Shelly, half anxious, half relieved. "Maybe he's not home."

Shelly walked up and down the wrap-around porch, hugging herself. Mr. Mayfield kept a very tidy house. The hedges lined the porch, trimmed perfectly. The wooden planks on the porch glistened with shiny paint.

Even his trees seemed well-kept with no mud splotches on the trunks. I stared at the tops swaying in the breeze as I pressed the doorbell again.

A voice called down from the trees.

It seemed to crawl from the heart of the

leaves, down the trunk and into my ears.

"Shelly Miller. Curtis Chatman. Don't move. Stay right where you are."

Startled, I strained to see where the voice came from.

Shelly nudged me and pointed at the tree at the front of the house.

A dark figure slid down the trunk. Judging from its small size, it couldn't be Stacy Calhoun. As it came hurriedly down the walk toward the front porch, I could see thick glasses glisten in the light from the pale-yellow porchlight.

It was Mr. Mayfield.

"I know why you're here."

He seemed pretty calm, almost casual. Too casual for somebody who had just slid down a tree in his front yard.

He looked from Shelly to me and back again. He acted as if he'd found us at school in the hall without a pass. Surely he couldn't keep up the old teacher-student thing out here at this time of night, especially after everything that happened today.

He continued past us with large strides. "Come inside," he said as he tugged at his tightly rolled sleeves, then tucked in his grass-stained shirt.

Shelly looked at me and shook her head not to go, her eyebrows scrunched into a small "v". I could tell she had lost her nerve and I couldn't blame her.

I watched Mr. Mayfield pause in his open front door. His little grey terrier poked its nose through the curtain-covered window beside it.

I looked at Shelly and shrugged. I had come too far to turn back now. I followed Mr. Mayfield through that door with a million questions in my mind.

I could see a very orderly living room off to the left and a dimly lit kitchen off to the right. The billowing curtains in the living room caught my eye. All the windows were open! A strange thing for a person to do when he knows he's being...

hunted.

Before I could say one word, Mayfield picked up the phone from a little table in the foyer.

He looked at me and then at Shelly as she closed the door behind her.

"Mr. Mayfield I..." I didn't have time to get out another word before he spoke into the phone. My blood ran cold.

"Mrs. Chatman? Yes. This is Mr. Mayfield. Curtis is here with me. Yes, Shelly, too." He chuckled.

He was talking to my mother. I couldn't believe it! He'd ratted on us!

I was dead!

"Okay. That won't be a problem. Think nothing of it. Okay, see you soon." He hung up.

I couldn't help it. I barked out, "I CAN'T BELIEVE IT! YOU JUST CALLED MY MOTHER! I'M DEAD!" I'd be lucky if I ever saw daylight again. Shelly just stood staring, her mouth open.

"Yes. She and your father are on the way to get you. She's going to tell your parents where you are, too, Shelly. It seems they've been searching for you two for over an hour." He marched into the living room and plopped into an overstuffed chair.

We followed him automatically.

My feet seemed to have a mind of their own as I entered the darkened living room.

No lights on. Only the cold light of the moon pouring through the open windows and spilling its pale blue glow all over the perfect grey carpet and Mr. Mayfield's outstretched body.

The grey terrier sprang up and into Mr. Mayfield's arms where it sat on his stomach. He scratched its ears as it yawned.

"You want to know what Mr. Calhoun and I were arguing over, don't you, Curtis?" he said matter-of-factly.

I nodded still trying to accept the fact that my parents were on their way over here and would kill me the very moment they arrived.

Shelly, thankfully, still had her voice. "We just wanted some answers, Mr. Mayfield. We didn't put all those bugs in that box, Mr. Calhoun did. I swear. This is totally unfair. He's out to get us! Why?" She twisted her ponytail nervously.

"You two saw the book, didn't you?" he said, still rubbing his terrier's head.

We didn't say anything.

"How much do you two know about were-wolves?" he asked. His eyes narrowed, cold and staring.

The dog also stared at us. The moonlight pouring through the large windows outlined its straggly grey fur.

We didn't say anything.

"Come here, Curtis." He sat up.

The dog groaned and wrestled as he held it firmly in his hands, his fingers moving toward its mouth. I stepped closer.

Mr. Mayfield's fingers spread the lips of his pet, revealing sharp pointy teeth.

"See there, how sharp they are? How solidly in place? He can put fifty pounds of pressure on each one of those little blades. Feel one." He held the dog firmly.

I hesitated, staring at the exposed teeth, sharp little blades glistening in the moonlight.

"Go on. Feel one," he insisted.

I reached out and placed the tip of my finger under the dog's pointy incisor.

It punctured the tip of the skin so easily, I didn't even feel it. I saw a dot of blood grow on my finger.

"This is a small dog, Curtis. A very small dog." I could feel his eyes pierce me as easily as that dog's tooth. "You didn't see me fight with anyone today. I didn't even meet with Stacy Calhoun. You two put the bugs in the box and you are very sorry."

I wanted to argue. I wanted to say he was completely wrong and he knew it. I wanted to ask him why he would lie and stick up for that creep, Stacy Calhoun. I wanted to tell him I would prove everything. But as I looked at him, I couldn't say a word.

His eyes were so full of fear at that moment, I thought he might cry.

He held my arm tightly. I knew he was serious. The dog left his lap as I eased from his grip and stepped away.

Shelly nervously backed into an end table as the doorbell rang.

Instantly, a hall light snapped on and Mr. Mayfield opened the door, laughing and talking to the two people standing there.

Everything after that happened in a daze. I couldn't really focus on anything. Everything Mr. Mayfield had said scared me. It had really scared me.

Mom and Dad came in looking happy to see me and ready to kill me at the same time.

Dad prodded Shelly and me onto the porch with the back of his hand as he thanked Mr. Mayfield. I didn't hear what they said and I really didn't care.

We walked to the car at the curb.

Mom apologized again to Mr. Mayfield for any trouble we'd caused. Dad agreed with her and promised it wouldn't happen again.

Shelly slid onto the rear seat of the car and scooted across.

I stared at Mr. Mayfield and that dog as I closed my door and rolled the window down.

Mr. Mayfield smiled and waved as the car pulled slowly away. Then I saw it. On his out-stretched, waving palm as plain as day.

Burned in the center of Mr. Mayfield's palm was a five pointed star, a pentagram!

The mark of the werewolf.

I stifled a scream and quickly rolled up the window.

15

I stared blankly at the back of Mom's head for what seemed like hours. Everyone seemed far away, like they were in a thick fog.

Shelly sat on her side of the car seat, neither of us talked for fear of my parents hearing. As a matter of fact, no one talked.

I felt a surge of unexplainable panic. I couldn't stand to look out the window but I couldn't stand looking around in the car either. I felt sick and claustrophobic. I wanted to stretch and try to shake that "closed in" feeling, but I knew that any movement would break the heavy silence.

My stomach churned, as if I'd ridden one roller coaster too many. I had to get out of the car. I needed time to think about what I'd seen and about what Mr. Mayfield told me. I needed to get some air. Now.

"Dad, I'm hungry. Can we please stop and get something to eat?" This ploy had to work. I tried to sound extra pitiful and I knew that even if it didn't work for Dad, Mom would fall for it. After a little crisis like this, there was only one sure fire way to get the family talking again.

"McDonald's is right around the corner. Maybe it wouldn't hurt if we got a little something." Mom patted Dad's hand.

Mom loved McDonald's. She'd hated it for a long time until I started baseball and piano. Then we fell into the habit of going there right after practice.

I could see the golden light of the arches ahead. It could have been anywhere and I wouldn't have cared.

I had to get out of the car.

Dad sighed as he parked. He slid easily between a Volvo and some little hatchback that pulled out beside us.

I opened my door and immediately felt better as a breeze hit my face.

Dad brought a tray with four burgers, one chicken sandwich, three fries and four drinks to our table against the window.

We stuffed our faces between sharp questions like... "Didn't you know we'd be worried sick?" Mom exclaimed.

"Do you two ever stop to think? What could be so important that it couldn't wait until tomorrow? Mr. Mayfield didn't get you in trouble, you know," Dad reminded us between gulps of orange soda.

Mom and Dad took it easy on me. They wouldn't yell at me with Shelly around. But once they dropped her off, they'd get their chance. Pacing themselves for later, I guess.

After a few more bites of burger, I felt braver. I decided I should be trying to make nice and soften Mom and Dad up a little before we got back home.

Yet, I couldn't stop thinking about Mr. Mayfield's palm, seared with that symbol, the pentagram, the mark of the werewolf!

I looked out the window at the near-empty parking lot and could have sworn I saw Mayfield's dog's teeth in the reflection on the glass.

Suddenly the window lit up with the

lights of a large pick-up pulling into the space in front of the window where we were eating.

The truck flew into the space! It looked like it COULDN'T STOP! Its lights froze us in our seats as it roared within inches of the glass!

"HOLY COW!" Dad cried. He almost jumped out of his seat.

The truck bounced to a stop and the lights shut off. We all breathed a sigh of relief. For a brief moment, the uncomfortable tension between us lifted.

"Crazy drivers. That's how people get killed. What if his brakes had failed? I'm going to say something to that guy," Dad growled.

I looked over at Shelly. She stared intently out the window as a look of horror crept across her face.

"Shelly?" I asked with a slight shiver.

Then I saw him.

I couldn't believe it.

I saw the driver close the door of his truck and walk in front of the bumper with long, slow steps.

Stacy Calhoun opened the door to the restaurant.

16

Stacy Calhoun marched through the glass doors of McDonald's like he owned the place. He looked from side to side with his nostrils flaring, like some kind of hunter.

Like a wolf.

I swallowed hard.

Then I almost choked because Mom waved and smiled at him. I couldn't believe it! Mom knew him?

"STACY!" she cried out cheerfully.

I tried to stop her. I even grabbed her arm to stop her frantic waving.

Too late. Mom, the social butterfly, was in full flutter.

Shelly looked at me, her eyes pleading for me to do something. I couldn't.

She started to slide down in her plastic,

yellow seat. Only the top of her blond head poked out above the table.

Stacy saw us and walked toward us, smiling. Mom stood up so fast, she nearly knocked the drink from my trembling hand. She seemed excited to see him.

"Stacy Calhoun! Come on over here. I haven't seen you in ages."

Dad cringed. Somehow I got the feeling that Dad didn't like this guy either.

Mom, Dad, and the former-quarterback-turned-terrorist-substitute exchanged brief accounts of their current activities, chatted about how long it had been since they had seen each other and about how they ought to get together sometime.

I sat there, trying not to look in his direction. Every word he said made my skin crawl, like the sound of fingernails on a chalkboard. Sheer torture.

Shelly's Mom and Dad knew this guy's creepy past. Why didn't my parents? They talked to him like they'd been friends since sixth grade.

I even heard Mom mention dinner at our house some night!

Suddenly I felt a large hand on my shoulder. I couldn't help but cringe.

"Hello, Curtis. No hard feelings I hope," the devil said, smiling.

I looked up at him and almost gasped.

The fine layer of blond hair that had covered his face before had grown thicker. Every strand was visible and his eyebrows had grown completely together. His eyes shone like steel mirrors.

I tried to talk but couldn't. Shelly kicked me under the table. She had been staring out of the window at his truck. She raised her eyebrows as if trying to say something.

"I think they're still a little embarrassed about the incident at school, Stacy," Dad said coldly.

"Oh well, that's all over now. I think they learned their lesson. Besides..." Stacy snapped his gaze away from me and peered at my Dad. "You can't say we never did anything like that when we were in school, can you, Bill?" Stacy chuckled and punched Dad in the arm.

Dad winced, visibly uncomfortable. He shifted in his seat.

"You guys knew each other in school?" I

asked. Shelly kicked me again.

"Oh, yes," Stacy replied with a smile. "We met after school on several occasions," Stacy laughed.

Thankfully a McDonald's employee interrupted before Dad's temper exploded.

"Excuse me, sir, but I'm going to have to ask you to move your truck. It's in a handicapped parking spot."

"All right. I'll move it!" Stacy snapped at the poor girl. He regained his composure as he apologized to Mom and Dad.

"Well, we'd better be going," Mom said. She handed Dad a tray and began gathering wrappers and cups.

I stood up quickly, ready to leave. Stacy placed his hand firmly on my shoulder.

"By the way," he whispered into my ear, "I just paid a little visit to your friend, Mr. Mayfield. I'm afraid he's going to need a substitute tomorrow."

Through the noise in my throbbing head, I saw Mr. Mayfield's dog's teeth and the dot of blood coming out of my finger. Over and over again.

Then I saw that terrible pentagram on

Mr. Mayfield's palm.

Mom and Dad were quietly chatting about Stacy's rudeness when Shelly kicked me again. Hard. I was ready to yell at her when I saw her nod toward the truck.

I looked out the window as Stacy reached the door.

In the back of the truck were the two large boxes from school.

It hit me like a flash.

I knew then what I had to do.

17

"I have to go to the bathroom!" I cried, running toward the restrooms.

"Slow down, Curtis! No running!" Mom yelled as I rounded the corner. Shelly must have known what I planned to do. She gave me a nod.

To the right of the restrooms was the door leading outside. I knew that once I went through that door, Mom and Dad couldn't help me anymore. I'd be on my own and taking my life in my hands.

I took a deep breath and slipped outside.

The sting of the cold night air surprised me. I crept up along the side of the building and stood against the wall. The buzzing fluorescent lights above me attracted tiny moths that fluttered around like snow.

I brushed a few away as I saw the truck

roll to a stop at the furthest parking spot in the parking lot.

He would have to pull way out there in the dark, of course.

Well, Mom and Dad would be less likely to notice me out there. Then again, if I got into *trouble* they would be less likely to notice me out there. Fine. I steadied my nerves and waited until I saw Stacy's hulking form disappear back inside the restaurant.

I went for the truck, hoping no one was watching.

I saw no other cars around and noticed the only parking lot light in the area had burned out.

The truck was incredibly tall. I couldn't even see in the darkened windows.

It didn't matter. I was after something in the back. I put my foot on the tire and climbed, landing with a soft thump in the back of the truck. The bed was wet with dew.

Toward the front sat two large boxes and a couple of full garbage bags.

I crept toward the boxes.

Somehow I knew those boxes, one taped

shut and other one open, probably held the answers to this puzzle.

I never even noticed the window in the back of the truck cab, a small black rectangle, half open.

As I reached the boxes, I smelled something very strange coming from that little window. With a blurring rustle of movement and a loud SNAP, the window filled with the snarling, snapping jaws of a large wolf!

The howls and barks made my heart stop and I felt the hot wind from its snout on my arm. From the dark of the cab glowed two little fierce coals.

I fell backward as rows of razor sharp teeth tried to chew their way out of that little black window.

It wanted to chew on me.

18

My hand darted again between the glistening fangs that snarled and gnashed at the air.

I cried and moaned softly but I had to reach that box even if it cost me my hand.

I pulled away again in time to feel the rush of air from its gaping mouth.

I could hear the snap of the jaws and the scrape of razor sharp claws on the window.

Sobbing, I reached toward the box.

It tumbled to its side and the book slid out with a loud thud. I grabbed it with both hands and jumped off the side of the truck.

The wolf in the truck cab ran back and forth on the seat, causing it to shake wildly from side to side.

From the corner of my eye and through the growing mist, I saw the same hulking figure that I'd seen before. The same one that tried to kill Shelly and me with the car.

I knew it was Calhoun.

I ran. I ran so fast and so hard, I almost didn't feel my feet touching the ground.

I ran straight to Mom and Dad's car and flung open the rear door.

In two seconds, I slammed the rear door and had it locked.

I lay down in the back seat, my chest heaving and my stomach in knots. I stashed the book under the front seat. I had never been so scared in my life.

I knew he was coming.

Any second now, I would hear the scraping of his claws on the door. I would feel the car rocking from his ponderous weight.

He would bound across the pavement and in two seconds, crash through the window, dragging me out by my feet and then...the door opened, and the light came on in the car.

I screamed!

"CURTIS! What is wrong with you!" Mom cried.

"Tell me you didn't cause all that commotion in the restaurant?!" Dad barked.

I blinked. I couldn't believe it. Only Mom and Dad and Shelly. I would live!

At least for the moment.

Shelly nudged me over and climbed into the back seat. "Did you see him?" she whispered. "I thought he came this way."

Dad started the car. "I thought you were going to the bathroom. We were waiting for you inside."

"Sorry," I mumbled, still shaking all over. "I didn't see you."

"Well, you better not have been in on that prank in there. It was not funny. Someone could have been hurt."

"Prank?" I asked, looking over at Shelly.

"Some kids made a horrible mess in there," Mom said. "I just feel bad for that manager. It'll take him all night to get it cleaned up."

Dad agreed. "Kids like that spoil everything for everyone else. It's not funny. When we were kids..."

I leaned over to Shelly as Dad rattled on about himself and his peers.

"I think I saw him. He chased me to the car," I whispered.

Shelly grabbed my hand. Her sweaty

hand trembled. Fear lowered her voice even more than before. Mom and Dad could not hear her.

"After he came back from moving his truck, he asked where you'd gone. They told him 'the bathroom' and he said 'oh' and walked off. I told your Mom and Dad I had to go too, so I could keep an eye on him for you.

"I rounded the corner, heading toward the restrooms, when I heard this angry howl and a slam! Like a stall door being slammed.

"Then it sounded like the walls of the bathroom were being pounded into rubble! The paintings on the wall outside the bathrooms all fell and shattered when they hit the ground.

"Then I saw *it*.

"From out of the men's room door burst this large, fur-covered thing that moved like a black shadow. It sprang with two leaps out the side door. Curt, it stood as tall as the ceiling!

"I screamed my head off.

"It had to be him, Curtis. It had to be Stacy Calhoun." Shelly had squeezed all the blood from my hand.

"He knows we're on to him. He'll be back. He'll come back to get it."

I pointed to the book under the seat. "But this time we'll be ready."

Just looking at the cover of the book I stole from Calhoun's truck gave me the creeps. This rotten book caused all the trouble in the library, but hopefully it could give me a clue to stop him.

I opened it.

In the first picture, a large, bearded man stood on a rock. He had crazy eyes and a long strand of drool coming from his mouth.

He held a large battle axe over his head as he screamed in anger.

He wore a wolf's skin.

According to the caption under the picture, Vikings or Norsemen of this type became known as *berserkers,* battle-crazed warriors who wore the skins of the animals they wanted to be like, usually a bear or a wolf.

Unstoppable in battle, they became nearly invincible as long as they wore their animal skins.

The book scared me because it was *real*. I could feel it.

I had been sentenced to spend my one day of suspension in my room. Fine with me. I had a lot of reading to do...and planning.

My eyes drifted back over to the irresistible book. It had a power about it. Like nothing I have ever felt before.

I had read plenty of books about monsters and all sorts of supernatural stuff and I'd seen more movies than you can count, but nothing like this.

The book itself made my bed sag, as if it were made of stone.

The pages seemed strange, leathery and tough.

I looked closely at the cover. The silver embossing, half a man's face and half a wolf's face, seemed to glow against the dark leather.

I opened the book again and flipped through the pages. I couldn't even look at some of the gross illustrations. I soon learned that I didn't know near as much as I thought I did about werewolves.

I picked the book up, placed it on my desk and snapped the light on.

Two o'clock in the afternoon. I didn't want to risk anyone seeing me with this book, so I had my curtains drawn.

I opened the book again.

A cold wind whistled through my room as I continued reading. The book seemed to read itself to me. I could hear another voice in my head reading the words.

There are three types of werewolves.
The first is the hereditary werewolf.
Their families are werewolves and they pass it down from generation to generation. They live in clans and don't associate with people much, unless they're hungry. They look like real wolves.
The second type is the benevolent werewolf or lycanthrope. They live alone and they received their powers accidentally, either through a bite or a curse. They hate their appearance and don't want anyone or anything to suffer because of

*their sickness. They are very sad and try every-
thing to cure themselves. The more they hate
their curse, the more human they appear when
they change. Some look completely human when
they're transformed. They merely act like a wolf.*

*The third type is the worst of all. The vol-
untary werewolf or loup-garou (loop-gar-oh).*

*They actually want to be werewolves and
go to great lengths to become one. They love the
power and they love to hunt. They use everything
from medallions to potions to change, even
magic. They always have a wolfskin that they put
on while in human form and when they want, the
skin melts into their own. They become a half-
man, half-beast, like the berserkers in the book.*

*Despite their differences, they do have
some similarities.*

Their attacks are almost always deadly.

*When in human form, they have a lot of
hair on their faces and hands, and usually their
eyebrows grow together.*

*Lastly, a pentagram will always appear
on the hand of their next victim.*

"Mr. Mayfield," I muttered.

I wondered if Mr. Mayfield had made it to

school today. I called his house. No answer. Had Stacy Calhoun made good on his threat?

I walked over to the window. Carefully I peered down my tree-lined street. I used to think that a werewolf could only come out on nights with a full moon.

Not true.

They could prowl any time they wanted. Wolfsbane didn't effect them either. It's only a flower, nothing more.

It would be dark soon. I closed the curtain again and started to pace.

My mind raced with all this new information and I became more scared with each passing moment.

I'd seen pictures in that book of what a werewolf can and will do if he gets a chance. None of them were pleasant. I didn't think I'd ever be able to sleep again.

I realized now that the problem was worse than I had thought.

The only way to get rid of a hereditary werewolf was by killing the whole family or clan with fire. Calhoun was the only one in town.

The only way to kill a lycanthrope was with silver. Touching them with silver would do it. In the middle ages, if you could slip a silver necklace over a lycanthrope's neck, he couldn't remove it and he would die.

It sounded like a super allergy. Like if you're allergic to bee stings, a single sting can kill you. I guess that's where the silver bullet story came from.

Stacy didn't seem like the sad or unhappy type to me. I couldn't be sure, though. What if the bully attitude was just a front?

The third one, the loup-garou, was the toughest to get rid of.

Almost nothing kills that one.

Not gunshots or knives or clubs or anything. Silver merely hurts a lot and so does fire. The only way, according to the book, was to find his wolfskin and sprinkle the inside with salt. When he put it on and began to transform, the salt would kill him and he would vanish.

Right. What were you supposed to do? Ask "Can I borrow your skin for a minute?" and then sprinkle it with salt and hand it back? I continued to read.

The skin could usually be found either on the werewolf's person or in his lair.

Pretty lame, I thought. Stacy would look

awfully strange running around with a wolf skin on.

I stood up and began to pace. The terrible tension made my head throb. I had to do something. Stacy knew I had his book and he would definitely want it back.

I had Shelly to worry about, too.

She called me in tears. Her palm itched terribly and wouldn't stop.

She said a symbol had appeared on it.

A pentagram.

She would be next.

Everybody treated us like celebrities at school the next day.

Some people told us that the library stunt would make us legends and they wished they'd had the nerve to attempt it.

Other people told us it was lame and we should grow up and not hurt other people. Yeah, we were celebrities, all right, but we didn't feel much like celebrating.

I met Shelly after third period in front of the walkway to the lunchroom. Everyone else had gone to stuff their faces. I knew I couldn't hold anything down if I tried.

"How you doing?" I asked, knowing the answer.

"I have a pentagram on my palm, you idiot. How are you doing? Brilliant question,

Curtis." She put up a brave front. "Do you have any idea how hard it is to hide something on your hand all day?"

"I got caught cheating that way once," I replied, making sure no one was around. "Did you bring what I asked you to?"

Shelly patted her pocket. "Yeah, I have them, for whatever good it will do."

"Let me see your palm."

I grabbed her hand.

She let it fall open. Her palm had turned a sickly black-purple, with the pentagram burned in deeply.

"Ouch. Does it hurt?" I touched it gently.

Shelly winced and pulled her hand away. "What do you think, you dork? It hurts like crazy. I'm scared, okay?"

"Did you find out anything about Mr. Mayfield?" I asked, changing the subject.

"Only that he didn't show up again. He wasn't here yesterday and he's not here today. He hasn't called in or anything." Shelly rubbed her palm. Her pale face and hollow eyes made it obvious that she hadn't slept.

"Stacy is here today, isn't he?" Once again, I knew the answer.

90

"His truck is." Shelly reached into her pocket. "Are you sure about this, Curt? It seems pretty risky."

"What other choice do we have? He knows I have the book. He'll come after you and then me."

Shelly pulled two objects from her pocket, two shiny, expensive looking silver earrings with very sharp edges.

"Did you file yours down?" I asked.

Without a word, Shelly pulled a piece of paper from her notebook and held it flat in front of my face.

I saw the tip of a razor-like earring poke through the paper and glide down, slicing through the paper. Shelly's dead serious face appeared on the other side.

Impressive.

The paper floated down to the ground in two pieces.

"I'll finish filing mine down during biology," I muttered.

The bell rang. Two periods to go.

22

The box sat on the desk, still taped shut, as it had been since I first laid eyes on it. I recognized it as the second box, the one we hadn't opened. The one I *didn't* get to in the back of his truck.

In front of the box, in front of the desk stood Stacy Calhoun. He seemed strangely at ease as he had since class first began. "Class, I have an announcement to make. I think Shelly and Curtis will find this especially interesting."

He adjusted his perfectly straight tie. His mouth pulled back in a smile.

Shelly and I smiled also, nervously, but we smiled nonetheless. As a matter of fact, the three of us took turns smiling at each other.

Shelly and I smiled because we each had in our pockets an ace in the hole, a trump card, our little secret weapons.

Mine had sliced my thigh in three different places between this period and last, and little spots of blood oozed through my jeans. I didn't care. It would be worth it. I sat ready. Scared but ready.

Shelly clenched her fist tightly and held it in her lap. She nodded at me.

Stacy Calhoun walked to the front of the class and clapped his hands together hard.

"Curtis Chatman and Shelly Miller, please come to the front of the room."

Shelly and I slid out from behind our desks. No matter how scared we felt, we couldn't let it show. We marched silently to the front of the class and stood in front of Stacy Calhoun.

"I wonder if you two would help me with my box," he said, as he pointed behind him.

We both looked at the taped, cardboard curiosity, then at each other and gulped.

"Please. Open it," he said.

I reached for the tape hanging loose from the end.

"Well? We're waiting," the teacher said, his voice mocking.

I started to pull the tape when Shelly's

hand stopped me.

"I'll do it, Curtis," she said.

"WAIT!" Stacy called. "The announcement first."

The whole class leaned forward.

"I am very pleased to announce that I will no longer be your substitute teacher."

Everyone looked at each other. A wave of relief swept across Shelly's face.

"I have just received notice that I'm to teach this class . . .permanently." He spun to look at us.

NO! My mind shouted and my mouth fell open. While the class applauded, Shelly groaned and pulled the tape off the box. The flaps fell open.

"Please hand those out, immediately." He practically skipped to the center aisle.

I looked down and saw a box filled with invitations. Dozens of invitations. This wasn't the same box at all! Not the same one we'd carried. Not the same one in the truck. Not the same one at all! Now that I looked at it, I saw it didn't even have the same label.

"Invitations?" Shelly said.

"YES! Invitations to the big party I am

giving for you and all your parents to celebrate my return to Fairfield and my new full-time teaching position. It will be at my house on Beechwood, near my father's old dog pound. Everyone must come."

Shelly and I trudged down the aisles passing out the invitations, giving lambs the tickets to their slaughter. I handed my friends, my classmates, the address of the big bad wolf. He might as well have had a walk-in oven.

I passed out my handful and went to the desk to get more, then paused at the box and looked back down the aisle. The kids buzzed excitedly about Mr. Calhoun's party.

Shelly handed out her last few at the back of the class. The clock signalled four minutes until the final bell.

Shelly looked up at me and without a word moved behind Mr. Calhoun. He had now moved to a spot exactly three desks up from the back, center aisle. I stood in front of his desk.

"Don't just stand there, Chatman. Get moving!" he barked.

The time had come.

Shelly reached up and dropped her silver, razor-like earring down Mr. Calhoun's back.

He let out a scream that ballooned into a full-fledged howl! He started to flop around, tearing at his shirt. Blood trickled down his back, making red splotches on the white cloth.

The desks around him tipped over as kids scrambled to the sides of the room. A fortunate few made it to the door.

Shelly quickly stepped back to the wall, as Mr. Calhoun ripped his shirt. A sudden, strange wind whipped around us, blowing the papers on the desks.

Mr. Calhoun grew! In front of our eyes, he grew so rapidly that his shirt tore away from his transforming body.

The hair on his body sprouted. His eyes

glowed red and seethed with anger. His voice became an animal's cry. His fingers had sprung small claws.

Instinct told me to run, but I swallowed hard and stood my ground.

He snarled and screamed in fury at the earring as it continued its merciless journey down his pants. He roared at Shelly, raising his clawed hands to strike!

"I KNEW IT! YOU'RE A WEREWOLF!" I yelled as loud as I could. I had to get his attention and it worked. He turned and glared at me.

He still looked more human than wolf, as if something had stopped him from changing completely.

I jumped behind his desk as he let out an ear-piercing shriek and lunged down the aisle toward me.

He bounded like a wolf.

Like the wolf in the science film.

This time the rabbit had a silver bullet.

I reached for the industrial strength slingshot I had fashioned the night before and loaded it with my silver beauty. It almost took my finger off. Razor sharp.

I braced my back against the wall and

faced the roaring, spitting monstrosity that barrelled down the aisle.

Then I noticed his stupid letterman's jacket hanging on the chair beside me.

It had a wolf's fur lining. A wolf's fur lining. A WOLF'S SKIN!

I let the earring go as he leaped. It flew through the air like a bullet and smacked him in the forehead with a loud THWACK!

He didn't stop.

I realized then ...

"IT DIDN'T WORK! I'M DEAD!"

I saw a mouth full of razor-sharp teeth and felt my hair blown back from the ancient wind of his lungs. I rolled to the side.

SMASH! He hit the chalkboard like a bombshell. It cracked and splintered right off the wall.

I thought he'd come after me, but instead, through the cloud of chalk dust and plaster, I saw him grab his fur-lined letterman's jacket and head to the side wall.

The principal and Coach Dawson plowed through the terrified kids in time to hear a thunderous splintering of glass and see a gaping hole in a window on the third floor.

Stacy Calhoun had gone.
And I knew where.

We slipped out of school during the confusion and beat it back to my house. Mom and Dad weren't home yet and I could only hope that the school hadn't called them at work to tell them what happened. I paced round and round the couch. Shelly had picked up the habit too.

"What do we do now? Why didn't the earrings work? Why isn't he gone!" she asked.

"He's a loup-garou. That's why it didn't work. Silver only hurts him. It doesn't k-kill him," I stammered.

"How do you know that?"

I slammed open the book to precisely the right page. The wind suddenly blew the window shut. "See? Right there. The only way to get rid of him is to pour salt inside his wolf skin."

"He doesn't have a wolf skin!"

"His letterman's jacket. It's lined with wolf fur!" I yelled.

"Well that's it then. We're dead. How are we going to get salt into his jacket? He's going to get me and then he's going to get you. What are we going to do?"

"Everyone's going to be looking for us. I'm not sure if everyone realized what happened. Do they know why we did what we did?" I asked. We paced faster and faster, and I felt a wave of nausea.

"Well, yeah. I only dropped a razor down his back, and you only hit him in the head with one! Everyone will think it's our f-fault again," she stammered, on the verge of crying. She paced in small circles, scratching her palm frantically.

I tried to calm her down. "Shelly, you're losing it. Everyone in class saw Stacy Calhoun turn into a werewolf. Now they know what he is. How could they blame that on us?" I asked.

"They saw us attack our teacher after he handed out party invitations, driving him right out the window!" she cried, scratching her palm harder now. "We'll be suspended for life this time!"

"Shelly! Get a grip! Listen to what you're saying! Look at your palm! A suspension is the least of your worries!"

She stopped pacing and looked at me, tears streaming down her cheeks. "Maybe if we give him the book back ..."

"Are you crazy?! That's our only defense!"

"We'll offer a trade. He can take his stupid book, and we'll keep our mouths shut as long as he doesn't hurt anybody," she said.

"What's to stop him? He'll just take the book and kill us anyway! We have to think. The answer has to be in the book, and we have to find it before he finds us."

"You're right," Shelly said, wiping her eyes. "What do we do?"

"I don't know." I really didn't. I couldn't think straight. My mind raced, but I kept coming up with complete blanks. I searched through the book, but found nothing.

Then it hit me.

"We'll just have to wait," I said.

Shelly shot me a puzzled look.

The phone rang. We looked at each other.

Oh man, it could be the principal. Worse, it could be my parents.

It rang again.

"Pick it up," Shelly demanded.

I watched it as it rang for a third time, hoping it would stop.

"Pick it up, Curt. It has to be important! It could be my parents, too."

It rang again.

I grabbed it.

"Chatman's residence."

The voice on the line chilled me. I nearly dropped the phone, staring at the wall in sheer, frozen horror.

Stacy Calhoun. His voice sounded different, barely understandable. But what he said rang crystal clear. I hung up and turned to look at Shelly.

"Who?" she asked.

"Calhoun. He said he'll see us tonight."

The bus hissed to a stop at the station. Several strangers filed past Shelly and me and found seats.

I would have traded places with any of them at this point. Thirteen years old and my life was about to end. There was so much I hadn't done yet. I was hungry, too. Ravenous.

I'd miss so many people. I thought about Mom and Dad. About my friends at school. I could only see them for a second in my head before they were shredded by sharp claws and slashing fangs.

This bus ride could be one way.

I knew it.

I looked at my watch. In about three hours, Shelly and I would either be slouching in these seats in relief, or we would be slowly digesting in the stomach of the big bad wolf.

"Shelly, pass the salt," I said.

She did. The blue cylinder of salt slid from her jacket and into my damp, trembling hands. I poured a little on my finger and touched it to my tongue.

"Don't worry," I said, trying to convince both of us. "This will all be over soon."

"That's what I'm afraid of," Shelly blurted.

I shut up and looked out the window. I checked my pockets again. Matches. Gum. Wallet. All there.

We couldn't just sit at home and wait for him to come and kill us. We both knew that. We had no place to hide. He would find us. The police wouldn't believe us and neither would our parents. Besides, he would tear through anyone to get to us. We decided to do what he would least suspect.

Shelly figured out where he would probably be. An obvious answer, but a smart one.

It said in the book that a loup-garou had a home like everyone else. He also had a lair, a place where he would take his victims to feed at his leisure. A place where he could hang his fur, or letterman's jacket as the case might be.

The bus slowed down again. Shelly and I both craned our necks to see exactly where we were.

The yellow street lights didn't make reading the street signs any easier. One more stop.

We both sat back again.

An elderly woman sitting across from us squinted her baggy eyes and gave us the once over. "Aren't you kids a little young to be out this late, alone?" she croaked. Out of her large floppy overcoat, a tiny little rat-like dog poked its head and licked its lips. They both waited for an answer.

"Yes, ma'am, we're going to the pound," I said.

"Dropping off or picking up?" she asked with a scowl.

"Dropping off," I said, with my hand on the container of salt.

The bus squealed to a halt and we stepped out of its safe, well-lit confines onto the cold, dark street. A light fog covered the area. The moon shone bright and full.

Beneath its brilliant, silvery light rested the shabby building that used to house a dog pound.

None of its filthy windows remained intact and its broken sign hung by one chain.

Old yellowed newspapers and oily rags littered its display windows.

Stacy Calhoun's father's dog pound.

"You first," I said half-joking.

Shelly took me up on it.

26

She had her nose pressed against the glass window by the time I reached her. She was breathing hard.

"Oh man, Curtis, do you see it?"

I strained my eyes to see through the dirty window. Newspapers and rags covered the floor. Then I saw it. I couldn't believe it. The elusive second box. And open!

Shelly grabbed me.

"It's the other box. The real one! It's open! And right there!" She sounded crazy with excitement.

We stood at the very verge of death and her curiosity would kill her.

"Shelly, no!" I whispered as she moved to the end of the window.

Before I knew it, she had slipped in

through an empty window pane and crept slowly through the newspapers on the floor. The box tempted her from the back of the window display, only a few feet away.

I peered nervously up and down the street. No one in sight. Not a soul.

Shelly had reached the box and reached out to touch the lid.

I could only watch and hold my breath.

She grabbed the box by the flap and dragged it ever so slowly closer.

I pressed my nose to the glass to get a better view. Shelly sat with her back to me, pulling things out of the box and looking at them. I tried to see what she had found, all the while watching and listening for anything unusual.

It looked like a bunch of old books. She continued to pull stuff out, her ponytail wagging with each swing of her arms. I could barely see her through the muck on the window.

She pulled out a bunch of old magazines...then a hat...no, a cap. Then an old grey uniform of some type...then a big overcoat. She paused, flipping the coat over. No fur-lining. All these things looked old. They had probably belonged to Calhoun's father.

Suddenly she spun around, slamming an old faded school picture against the window, her eyes bulging!

She held an old picture of a football team. I looked at it for a moment before I recognized the players: Stacy Calhoun and Douglas Mayfield, arms around each other's shoulders and smiling like best friends. My biology teacher and the substitute. . .

the werewolf.

I looked at Shelly as she tried to mouth something to me through the glass. Her mouth formed words, but I didn't understand.

Something else grabbed my attention.

I frantically motioned for her to turn around.

A big, hairy shape rose up behind her, slowly, making her look very small. Its fangs dripped like faucets.

Its two yellow eyes snapped open.

I screamed as Shelly jumped over the display window wall and into the darkness of the dog pound. The large hairy form of a wolf looked at me for a moment in the moonlight, then plunged after Shelly.

It wasn't Calhoun, but the wolf from the truck. I could hear Shelly scream.

Without thinking, I ran to the door and broke inside. The darkness enveloped me and I couldn't see a thing.

"CURTIS! LOOK OUT!" Shelly cried.

As my eyes adjusted, I saw the wolf poised where she had fallen. It snarled at me and SPRANG!

For an instant, I recalled that science film of the wolf and the rabbit. I cried out and rolled to the side.

With a loud clang, the wolf plunged head-long into one of the empty cages on the wall. It tossed its head in a blood curdling yowl. I kicked at the door, which locked with a loud metallic whoosh, just as its teeth snagged my pants. He tore my ankle wide open. Blood soaked into my sock.

Shelly ran over to help me.

Then we saw the jacket.

It lay in the middle of the room, spread out neatly and turned inside out.

The fur lining glistened in the moonlight that streamed through the windows.

Trash and bones surrounded us, except in the area immediately around the jacket. Someone purposefully cleaned out a place for it...and for us.

It had to be the most obvious trap I'd ever seen.

What else could we do?

We looked at each other for a moment, then went for it, the salt container open in my hand.

Getting traction on the newspaper and

trash proved difficult.

Just before we reached the jacket, I felt my feet leave the floor. Someone lifted us off the ground.

Stacy Calhoun held us by the backs of our shirts, laughing and howling in delight.

His shirt hung in cotton tatters on his heaving chest. His eyes glowed blood red, and hair covered his huge, rippling body. His pointy ears twitched.

"My two star pupils! So glad you could come!" His voice sounded like a whole pack of animals growling at once.

We screamed as he flung us across the jacket and into the far wall. Shelly landed hard and cried out in pain, holding her arm.

It sounded as if she'd broken it.

I hit an old wooden chair that splintered into my knee like hot needles.

The salt container flew from my hand and rolled near Shelly. We both saw it lying between us, still closed, but it didn't matter. Too far to reach now. We'd blown it good.

I couldn't turn around. I knew he was coming for us. I could feel pain coming with hot breath and dripping teeth. My mind reeled. Only one thing to do.

I grabbed a stick from the broken chair, and, sobbing, wrapped an oily rag around it.

"You kids make yourselves at home while I slip into something more comfortable," Stacy Calhoun cackled as he reached for the jacket.

I turned to him with as much courage as I could muster.

I fumbled with the book of matches.

Anger washed over me. He would kill Shelly and me. He'd already broken her arm.

The torch blazed to life at the touch of the match in my trembling hand. I held the burning torch, and steadied myself, staring at him.

His huge burning eyes glued to it in fear.

"FETCH!" I yelled and threw the fiery stick as hard as I could.

"NOOO!" the Stacy thing cried as it leaped up to stop the flaming missile.

It slipped past him and flew through the air. I knew it wouldn't kill him, but it might at least distract him long enough for us get out of there in one piece.

It landed in the window where the box, the newspapers and oily rags immediately went up in a blaze. Flames licked the ceiling, filling the room with smoke.

He frantically scrambled to the window to put it out, to save his lair and his father's last possessions.

An opening at last!

The jacket lay there...wide open. I felt my legs go out from under me.

NO! I had to reach it. No matter what. Too close to give up now!

Shelly fell back against the wall as I grabbed the salt container and scrambled forward.

A wall of smoke blew over us in great brown billows.

Shelly screamed as I ran toward the middle of the room, pouring a fistful of salt into my shaking hand.

My heart jolted against my ribs as I choked in the clouds of smoke.

My mind numbed with terror. He would kill me before I reached the jacket.

I had to block it all out. The razor claws of the hideous Stacy Calhoun, the choking smoke, the roaring fire.

Smoke drifted around me and I saw the jacket in front of me, inches away!

I could reach it!

I had to reach the jacket before. . .

he did.

I heard a deafening roar and felt a tremendous sledgehammer blow to my back. A bulldozer of a hand scooped me into the air and sent me sprawling toward the window.

My hand opened as I tumbled!

Salt fell from my outstretched palm and vanished below.

The jacket disappeared from sight.

I hit the floor and cried out.
My mind reeled with disbelief.
I had missed the jacket.
The salt had vanished.
All hope had vanished.

Through the smoke and my stinging tears, I saw Stacy Calhoun's arms poking into the sleeves of his jacket.

He grew a full ten inches into the most horrifying, wolf-like thing I could have imagined. His shoulders had to be six feet across, and hunched, like an animal's. Pointed ears grew up the sides of his head like antennae.

In a cloud of smoke, it seemed to vanish for a moment.

Suddenly his hideous wolf-like head lunged through the smoke. Its piercing, mirror-like eyes froze me. I saw rows and rows of razor sharp fangs about to close around my head. I could practically feel them pierce my skin. My entire body blazed with shock! I blacked out for a moment before my eyes snapped back open.

I WAS DEAD!

Then the jacket hit the ground and Stacy Calhoun began to melt. His face bubbled and reddened. The grains of salt that stuck on his skin sank into small pits and ballooned into gaping holes.

With a final hideous shriek, Stacy Calhoun vanished.

I sat there for a second, unable to believe that I was alive. The salt must have landed in the jacket. I had done it.

I laughed out loud.

Then, through the smoke I saw an exhausted Shelly stagger toward me. Her blackened, tear-stained face twisted with agony and relief.

We had won.

The only things louder than the sounds of our feet against the pavement that night were the distant sirens and the howling. . .

of a wolf.

Shelly hadn't broken her arm. She only sprained it.

We managed to sneak home and clean up without our parents seeing us, and we only got in trouble for skipping school.

The police thought Stacy Calhoun had gone crazy in class and torched his Dad's old place. They're still looking for him. It seems they've been looking for him for a long time.

As for me, well, right now I'm waiting for Shelly to come over. I marked our place in the book.

It's almost midnight now and the moon is full and bright. The trees blowing outside haven't a leaf left on them. A cold wind keeps whipping through my room.

My palm is really hurting now and the

pentagram is almost fully formed. It itches like crazy, like Shelly said hers did before it went away.

Stacy Calhoun didn't come to Fairfield to get away from his family, his clan.

He wanted to add to it.

I have a gut feeling Mr. Mayfield is coming to see me tonight and well...

I have some reading to catch up on.

And now
an exciting preview
of the next

2 The Midnight Game

by Johnny Ray Barnes, Jr.

1

"C'mon, Tyler," I said to myself. "There's nobody out there. You're the only one left on this football field."

I heard the words leave my mouth, but I didn't believe them. From my seat at the top row of the bleachers, I could see the whole field. Something definitely moved on the other side of the field; the dark side. I could swear someone was staring at me from those shadows.

Football practice had ended. The sun had almost gone down, and Dad was going to be late picking me up. And I felt sure someone was watching me from across the field.

The wind picked up and I began to wonder, for the millionth time, why I bothered with football at all. I don't like it that much. I play because of Dad. He wants me to learn something about playing on a team.

The only thing I'd learned so far was that something in the dark was watching me and it could come get me at any moment.

I stared until my vision went fuzzy. Was that something moving?

"Hey!" I yelled in my meanest voice. "I see you! I may be a kid but that doesn't mean I'm scared! Actually, I'm pretty brave!"

Then my heart stopped.

A ragged, dusty figure dragged its way from behind the broken wooden bleachers on the opposite side of the field. A hat, dark glasses, and a red scarf hid his face. His clothes were grungy brown, dirty looking. A cloud of dust flew off him with every step. The wind picked it up and swirled it, like a dust devil come to life.

He slowly climbed a row or two up the bleachers, then sat with his hands crossed in his lap and his back straight. He looked right at me.

My heart pounded. Sure, I thought something had been over there, but I didn't really believe it. Not really. It was one thing to imagine somebody out there, but this guy looked real. Were there be more like him? If I jumped from the bleachers and ran, could I get away?

Neither of us moved. I stared so intently my eyes ached. The cold wind stung my cheeks and made my eyes water. As I blinked to clear my vision, the dusty man moved.

He dug into his coat pocket. I couldn't see clearly, but it looked as if he pulled something out and laid it down beside him.

Whatever it was, he left it. He climbed down off the bleachers, and the dust cloud around him thickened. I may have been going crazy, but there seemed to be less of him than before.

He made his way around the stands, and disappeared into the dark.

I sat and stared for a long time. I looked where the figure had walked away, then back again at where he'd been sitting, and where he had left the...thing.

I was terrified, but I had to know what it could be.

I crept down with a lump in my throat and a knot in my stomach. The wind was so strong it nearly blew me off my feet. Trees outside the stadium swayed, as if warning me to go back.

I crossed the field slowly, keeping watch in every direction to make sure nothing came after me. The grass seemed to grab at my ankles. Finally, I made it to the other side.

I looked through the bleachers first, afraid something might grab my legs as I started climbing up. Nothing there. I looked, but didn't see anything. Crossing my fingers for good luck, I started up the stands.

The wind was so strong it nearly blew me off my feet. As I neared the spot where the man had been sitting, I could see something fluttering in the wind. A spider web. I climbed quickly past it, and found the mysterious object.

A small rock. A rock. I risked my neck crossing the field for a rock? But wait a minute. There was something was else under the rock...a ticket?

Yes, that's what it was. Worn and faded, but still readable.

"Green Devils vs. Mohawks 12:00 A.M. November 28, 1995."

Midnight? What kind of football team plays at midnight?

November 28, 1995 was tomorrow! The ticket looked older than me, but it had tomorrow's date!

Suddenly, a hand grabbed my shoulder and I screamed.

About the Authors

Marty M. Engle and **Johnny Ray Barnes Jr.**, graduates of the Art Institute of Atlanta, are the creators, writers, designers and illustrators of the **Strange Matter**™ series and the **Strange Matter**™ **World Wide Web page.**

Their interests and expertise range from state of the art 3-D computer graphics and interactive multi-media, to books and scripts (television and motion picture).

Marty lives in La Jolla, California with his wife Jana and twin terror pets, Polly and Oreo.

Johnny Ray lives in Tierrasanta, California and spends his free time with his fiancée, Meredith.